Captain McGrew Wants

YOU for his Crew!

Mark Sperring

Ed Eaves

BLOOMSBURY

LONDON OXFORD NEW YORK NEW DELHI SYDNEY

Meet Captain McGrew:
He's in need of a crew
to do all those jobs
that pirate crews do.

HELP
WANTED
Could THIS
be the job
for YOU?

You'll need bulging muscles
(strong fingers, strong thumbs)
to HOIST up the main sail
and wave . . .

You **HAVE** to be tough,
that has to be said,
to **PULL up** the anchor
from the sea bed . . .

You mustn't be little

and you mustn't be **BIG**,

but just the right size to

GET UP THAT RIG!

You MUST be prepared to SHOUT:

LAND AHOY!

And go by the title of

LAD,

LASS

or **BOY!**

Are you good
with a spade?

Do you complain if you're HOT?

Can you dig for **LONG** hours while others . . .

CANNOT?

And while Captain McGrew
sits in the cool shade,
can you make him a snack
and **SQUEEZE** lemonade?

Can you **H-EE-EE-AVE** out the treasure all by **YOURSELF?**

And **HAUL** it aboard
without **ONE** ounce
of **HELP**?

Can you SPLOOSH down
the POOP DECK?

BATTEN the
HATCH?

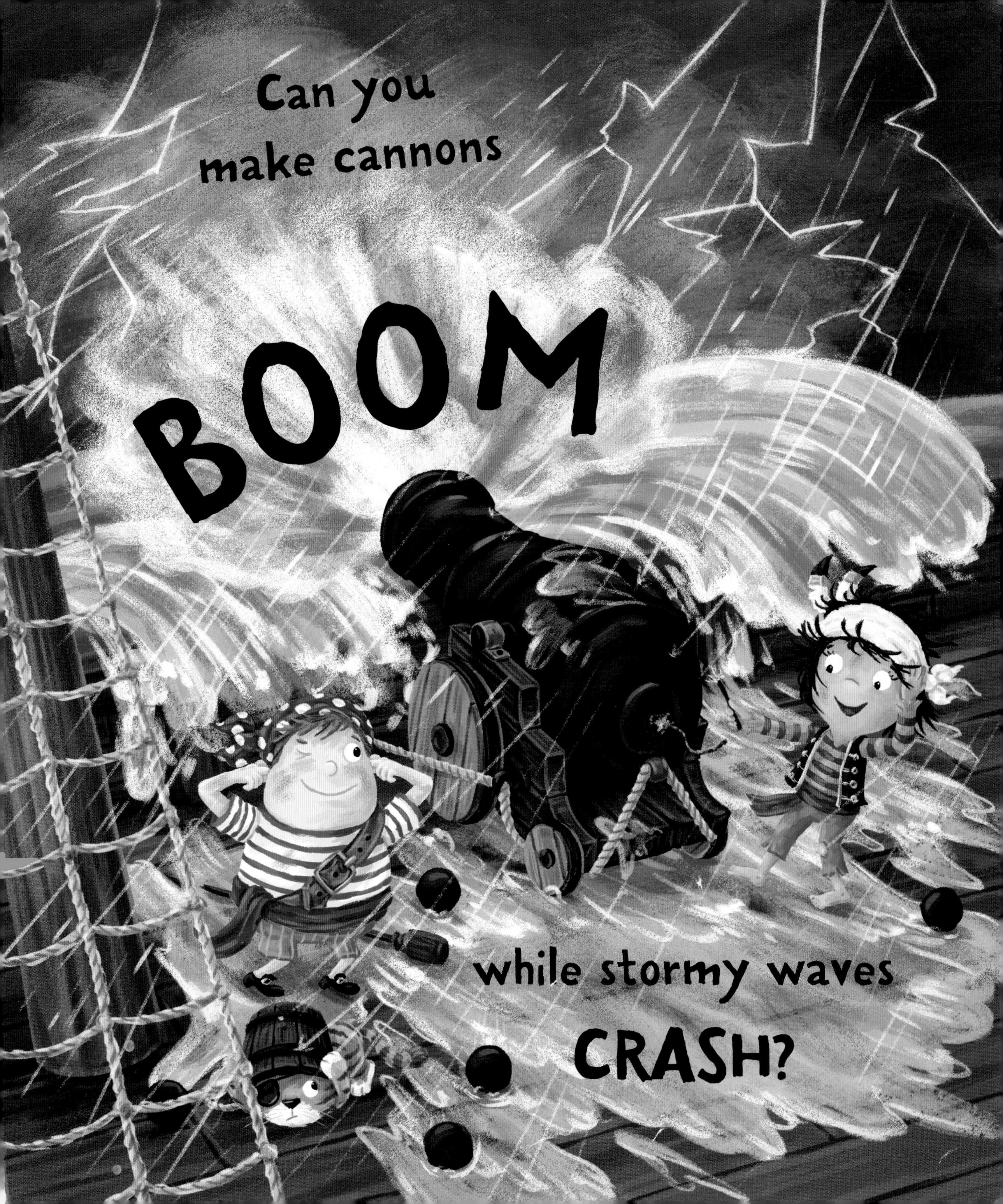

Can you
make cannons

BOOM

while stormy waves
CRASH?

And though you're plum tired, YES, after all THAT,
could you go to the galley and heat up a vat?

Then **RUSTLE** up supper
for Captain McGrew.
Something so simple . . .

like **OCTOPUS STEW?**

Would you **DO THE DISHES**
with no word of thanks?

Or grab hold of a broom and
start **WALKING THE PLANK?**

Could you clean off the hull, . . .
till it's tidy and neat?

And NEVER,

NO NEVER,

find time for a sleep?

Can you read bedtime stories?

Sing sweet songs you know?

Navigate through the night
as McGrew snores below?

I hope you **CAN** do this,
YES, REALLY, I do,
for I know a pirate who's
picked out his crew . . .

And

SHIVER-ME-TIMBERS

(uh-oh)

IT'S YOU!

YES, Captain McGrew

wants YOU

for his crew!

But for those who **AREN'T** suited to a life on the waves . . .

there's a knight here
called Norman
who's been looking
for knaves!